KIDS CAN'T STOP READING
THE CHOOSE YOUR
OWN ADVENTURE® STORIES!

"Choose Your Own Adventure is the best thing that has come along since books themselves."
—Alysha Beyer, age 11

"I didn't read much before, but now I read my Choose Your Own Adventure books almost every night."
—Chris Brogan, age 13

"I love the control I have over what happens next."
—Kosta Efstathiou, age 17

"Choose Your Own Adventure books are so much fun to read and collect—I want them all!"
—Brendan Davin, age 11

And teachers like this series, too:
"We have read and reread, worn thin, loved, loaned, bought for others, and donated to school libraries our Choose Your Own Adventure books."

CHOOSE YOUR OWN ADVENTURE®—
AND MAKE READING MORE FUN!

Bantam Books in the Choose Your Own Adventure® Series
Ask your bookseller for the books you have missed.

#1 THE CAVE OF TIME
#2 JOURNEY UNDER THE SEA
#4 SPACE AND BEYOND
#5 THE MYSTERY OF
   CHIMNEY ROCK
#22 SPACE PATROL
#31 VAMPIRE EXPRESS
#38 SABOTAGE
#39 SUPERCOMPUTER
#43 GRAND CANYON ODYSSEY
#44 THE MYSTERY OF URA SENKE
#45 YOU ARE A SHARK
#46 THE DEADLY SHADOW
#47 OUTLAWS OF
   SHERWOOD FOREST
#48 SPY FOR GEORGE
   WASHINGTON
#49 DANGER AT ANCHOR MINE
#50 RETURN TO THE CAVE OF TIME
#51 THE MAGIC OF THE UNICORN
#52 GHOST HUNTER
#53 THE CASE OF THE SILK KING
#54 FOREST OF FEAR
#55 THE TRUMPET OF TERROR
#56 THE ENCHANTED KINGDOM
#57 THE ANTIMATTER FORMULA
#58 STATUE OF LIBERTY
   ADVENTURE
#59 TERROR ISLAND
#60 VANISHED!
#61 BEYOND ESCAPE!
#62 SUGARCANE ISLAND

#63 MYSTERY OF THE SECRET
   ROOM
#64 VOLCANO!
#65 THE MARDI GRAS MYSTERY
#66 SECRET OF THE NINJA
#67 SEASIDE MYSTERY
#68 SECRET OF THE SUN GOD
#69 ROCK AND ROLL MYSTERY
#70 INVADERS OF THE
   PLANET EARTH
#71 SPACE VAMPIRE
#72 THE BRILLIANT DR. WOGAN
#73 BEYOND THE GREAT WALL
#74 LONGHORN TERRITORY
#75 PLANET OF THE DRAGONS
#76 THE MONA LISA IS MISSING
#77 THE FIRST OLYMPICS
#78 RETURN TO ATLANTIS
#79 MYSTERY OF THE SACRED
   STONES
#80 THE PERFECT PLANET
#81 TERROR IN AUSTRALIA
#82 HURRICANE!
#83 TRACK OF THE BEAR
#84 YOU ARE A MONSTER
#85 INCA GOLD
#86 KNIGHTS OF THE ROUND
   TABLE
#87 EXILED TO EARTH
#88 MASTER OF KUNG FU
#89 SOUTH POLE SABOTAGE
#90 MUTINY IN SPACE

#1 JOURNEY TO THE YEAR 3000 (A Choose Your Own Adventure Super
   Adventure)
#2 DANGER ZONES (A Choose Your Own Adventure Super Adventure)

MUTINY IN SPACE

BY EDWARD PACKARD
AND R.A. MONTGOMERY

ILLUSTRATED BY HOWARD BENDER

A Packard/Montgomery Book

BANTAM BOOKS
NEW YORK · TORONTO · LONDON · SYDNEY · AUCKLAND

RL 5, IL age 10 and up

MUTINY IN SPACE
Bantam Book / April 1989

*CHOOSE YOUR OWN ADVENTURE® is a registered trademark of Bantam
Books, a division of Bantam Doubleday Dell Publishing Group, Inc. Registered
in U.S. Patent and Trademark Office and elsewhere.*
Original conception of Edward Packard
Cover art by Richard Hescox
Interior illustrations by Howard Bender

ISBN 0-553-27854-1

Published simultaneously in the United States and Canada

---

*Bantam Books are published by Bantam Books, a division of Bantam Doubleday
Dell Publishing Group, Inc. Its trademark, consisting of the words "Bantam
Books" and the portrayal of a rooster, is Registered in U.S. Patent and Trademark
Office and in other countries. Marca Registrada, Bantam Books, 666 Fifth Ave-
nue, New York, New York 10103.*

PRINTED IN THE UNITED STATES OF AMERICA

O   0 9 8 7 6 5 4 3 2 1

MUTINY IN SPACE

WARNING!!!

Do not read this book straight through from beginning to end. These pages contain many different adventures you may have when you sign on as an apprentice aboard a spaceship. From time to time as you read along, you will be asked to make choices and decisions. Your choices may lead to success or disaster.

The adventures you have will be the result of your choices. After you make a choice, follow the instructions to see what happens to you next.

Think carefully before you make a move. When the other crew members aboard the *Baruna* stage a mutiny, you must decide whether to join them or stay with the captain of the spaceship. Your decision could mean either being trapped in space forever or becoming a hero!

Good luck!

For almost as long as you can remember, you've wanted to travel on a spaceship. At last you have your chance.

You signed on as an apprentice aboard the space transport *Baruna*. The day before lift-off, you meet Captain Philip Tyler, a short, heavyset man with dark hair.

"It will be a long, hard voyage." Captain Tyler glares at you, as if to see whether you're tough enough to make the trip.

"But you may be lucky," he adds. "We'll be taking on a cargo of palma fruit seeds that will fetch a pretty price on Earth—and, even young as you are, you stand to share in the profits."

"I'm glad of that, sir," you say respectfully.

You smile at him, but Tyler's face turns dark. "I said you *may* be lucky."

He strides off, leaving you to wonder if the rumors you've heard about his harshness and cruel, erratic behavior are true.

Turn to page 114.

2

Standing beside Jack Barnes, you watch Captain Tyler and the two crew members who have chosen to go with him enter the shuttle craft. They sit inside it but make no move to close the hatch.

Barnes prods your back. "Lock them in the shuttle. I want you to prove you're one of us."

You're in a terrible dilemma. If you refuse to obey Barnes, and the captain somehow survives, you'd probably be judged innocent if the mutineers are captured. On the other hand, if you cross Barnes by refusing to close the hatch, you risk everything, for your future is now in his hands.

If you obey Barnes's command to close the hatch, turn to page 9.

If you refuse, turn to page 22.

You quickly erase all evidence of the message. The mutineers continue in their lighthearted, swaggering ways as the *Baruna* speeds toward Genthe. Only you know that the Federation battle cruiser *Medea* will be there to meet you.

The next day at noon, local Genthe time, the *Baruna* glides through the troposphere and sets down on one of the broad, grassy plains near base Alpha, the only Federation station on this primitive planet.

You're hardly on the ground when a supersonic boom announces the imminent arrival of the battle cruiser *Medea*.

Barnes's face turns white as he watches the armed ship set down almost alongside the *Baruna*. "I didn't dream any other Federation ships would be here, much less a battle cruiser!"

"This is Admiral Mathis." A voice comes over the radio speaker. "Greetings to Captain Tyler."

"Good grief!" Fenton cries. "Can't we get out of here?"

Mumford shakes his head. "No way."

Turn to page 16.

Three months have passed since the *Baruna* left Earth. And how you wish you were back home! The ship has encountered one difficulty after another. And the strain of the long voyage has worn everyone down—Captain Tyler, most of all.

One evening, while the ship is passing through the Altair system, he summons everyone to the wardroom. His face is red—and the veins stand out on his neck.

"Who took them?" He shouts the words, though no one is more than ten feet away.

"Took what, sir?" Jack Barnes asks, his face breaking into a smile.

Tyler stares at him, then at each of the crew—Nan Pacella, Tim Fenton, the communications officer, Sam Mumford, the science officer, Ralph Kronick, the engineer, Bob Walker, the helmsman, and finally—you. He lowers his voice, but it's still laden with fury. "Someone here knows what I'm talking about—the vitro bars! They were to be saved until we got past Deneb. *Speak up, I tell you!"*

Turn to page 104.

Jack Barnes scowls when you tell him about the message. He follows you to the communications center, scans the computer screen, and returns quickly to the workroom.

"Quiet!" he yells, silencing his crew. You watch their faces—showing first annoyance and then fear as Barnes tells them about the dispatch. Everyone starts talking at once.

"Shut up, so I can think!" Barnes yells.

"Can't we land on the other side of Genthe?" Fenton whines. "They'd never know we were there."

"Stupid!" Barnes's voice is scornful. "You're a communications officer. Don't you have any idea of the kind of sensors they have? We'll have to find someplace else."

Mumford, who had been standing off to one side, now joins the others. "Look, Barnes," he says. "We have neither the fuel nor the food supplies to go cruising all over the galaxy. The nearest known star system with habitable planets is Ceres. It lies at least twenty parsecs beyond Genthe. It's too risky to try to reach it. We have two options— take our chances on Genthe or return to earth."

"They'll catch us either way," Fenton puts in.

Go on to the next page.

The others look anxiously at Barnes. For a moment he seems baffled. Then he stands more erect—you can see he's trying to be a strong leader. "We're not going to Genthe and we're not going back to Earth. We're going to find our own planet—there are a lot of them out there. And if we don't, we'll make it to Ceres! Is that understood?"

Turn to page 52.

"I'll go with the captain!" you say finally. "You're wrong, Barnes; and what's more, I think you're a crook. You're just using the ion storm as an excuse. I think you've been planning to steal the *Baruna* all along." The words rush out of your mouth before you can stop them.

"You've shown courage," Captain Tyler says softly. "I need people like you, but it could mean your life."

"Fool!" Barnes snaps at you, shoving you toward the shuttle.

Nan Pacella is standing silently by the door to the shuttle. Walker is already inside, seated in the copilot's seat. He's nervously readying the craft for departure.

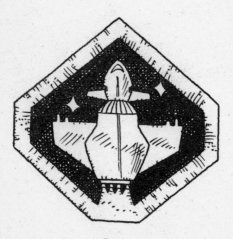

Turn to page 106.

Avoiding Captain Tyler's eyes, though you know he's looking straight at you, you seal the shuttle's hatch. You can't save the captain, anyway. Jack Barnes is captain now, and you'll only be digging your own grave if you start crossing him.

"You're one of us now!" says Barnes as he pats you on the back. A titanium door slides down, sealing off the space shuttle from the rest of the ship. Moments later you hear the exterior hatch open—then a muffled roar, and you feel the ship shudder as the shuttle is jettisoned into cold, black space.

"Full speed to Genthe," Barnes orders, and the *Baruna* lunges forward, accelerating to three-quarter light speed.

Turn to page 12.

Weeks pass as you cruise through space. Scan after scan on the radiation monitor turns up nothing. Barnes has set a course for the Ceres system, which has been reported to have several Earth-sized planets. The only problem is that Ceres is in a cluster of stars that is receding from Earth at over a hundred miles a second.

Desperately, you try to find a closer planet. Again and again you sense Barnes's presence behind you as you sit turning the scanners. More than once he asks, "Haven't you found something yet?"

You pick up a few red and brown dwarf stars, but, as far as you can tell, none of these suns have planets. They give out so little heat that any planet warm enough to live on would have to be very close by—not more than a few million miles from its sun. Each time you pass near one of these dwarfs, you search for planets—and each time you find nothing. A perfect planet may lie hidden on the other side of any of these dim stars, but the *Baruna* can't use precious time and fuel to double back and find out. The odds are too much against it.

Turn to page 59.

"I think we should go for the brown dwarf," you tell Barnes. Even as you're speaking, you're struck by waves of doubt. No habitable planet has ever been found in the vicinity of a brown dwarf. You realize your recommendation was based more on a hunch than on scientific analysis. But it's too late now. Barnes has already given the order. The only thing you can do is slip into your restraints and absorb the extra g-forces as the ship decelerates.

Steady on its new course, the *Baruna* streaks silently toward the little brown sun. The tension rises. No one speaks for long periods, but you have no trouble guessing what everyone is thinking—that the *Baruna* has been wasting precious fuel because of you!

"It's not a brown dwarf, it's a *black* dwarf!" Fenton blurts out.

Glancing at the optical scanner, you see what caused him to panic. The dwarf star is now close enough to appear as a disc, yet it can't be seen even though it has begun to eclipse stars behind it.

Turn to page 72.

Once the ship has settled on course, Barnes orders everyone to the wardroom. The mutineers break out bottles of rum and drink heartily in celebration of their daring feat. Several of them fall asleep as others become increasingly drunk. If the ship encounters a meteor storm or magnetic flux, you'll be the one who has to pilot the *Baruna* through it, you realize. These men are taking more risks than Captain Tyler did!

As the mutineers laugh and joke with each other you have a chance to observe them while they're off guard. Jack Barnes taunts the others constantly. It's clear now what a bully he is. Kronick, the engineer, is no better. A lean, hard man with a bristly red beard, he keeps boasting about how he will strip the Gentheans of "everything worth taking." Tim Fenton, the hot-tempered communications officer, jokes with the others, but there's a sullen look on his face that tells you he's brooding about something. Not a man to trust, you decide.

Mumford, the science officer, takes you aside.

"Watch out for these blokes," he says. "It may be we would have been better off drifting in space with Captain Tyler."

You nod in agreement and move to the communications center.

Turn to page 46.

Barnes nervously fingers the weapon, and impulsively you lash out and grab it out of his hand. The two officers seize him. A moment later other officers swarm aboard, and Fenton, Kronick, and Mumford quickly surrender.

As the others are led off, you wonder what will happen to you.

"Don't worry," Admiral Mathis says as he drapes a big hand over your shoulder, "We know the whole story. Captain Tyler and the others were rescued by a Federation explorer. They're fine. I'll see you're only placed on probation. You see, you may have saved my life. There are no force neutralizers—I was bluffing."

The End

"I think we should bypass this dwarf and set a course for Ceres," you say.

"O.K.," Barnes says, "I'll follow your advice."

The *Baruna* is soon established on its new course, but after two days, sensors report massive ion storms in the vicinity of Ceres. Maneuvering to avoid them would take more fuel than you have. You're about to report this to Barnes when you discover an Earth-sized planet orbiting Polaris, the North Star. The planet, which you name Katar, is about ninety-six million miles from Polaris, almost the same distance the Earth is from the sun!

If you recommend heading for Katar, turn to page 25.

If you recommend turning back and heading for Genthe, as originally planned, turn to page 90.

Three weeks have passed. You and the other mutineers are still in custody at Federation base Alpha on Genthe. You're going to be court-martialed; and if convicted, sentenced to exile for life on the asteroid Zircon. Word has come that, through great good fortune, Captain Tyler and the others have been rescued. He will testify at the proceedings.

You've hired a lawyer to defend you. After telling him what happened aboard the *Baruna,* you ask him what will happen to you.

He looks at you intently a moment, then says, "That all depends on what you did when Barnes's ordered you to close the hatch of the shuttle on Captain Tyler. If you obeyed Barnes, you'll be convicted with the others. If you refused to obey Barnes, you'll be found innocent."

The End

The cheer that went up as the ship settled safely on the ground reminded you of the jubilation that occurred after the captain and his followers were set adrift in the shuttle craft. Now, as then, the mood quickly turns somber. You all realize that your problems are far from solved.

The *Baruna* has landed on a broad plain near Alpha's equator. As far as the eye can see are broad steppes—treeless grasslands—and scrub forest. Ponds and small lakes lie in the hollows, and the landscape is speckled with massive outcroppings of granite and quartz. No animals, birds, or people are in sight.

"And this is the nicest place on the planet?" Kronick says ruefully.

"At least the ship's intact," Barnes says. "We don't have enough fuel to go anywhere in it, but it will serve us as a base camp. With any luck at all we'll find food, clothing, and shelter."

While Barnes is talking, Mumford, who had returned to the ship for a warmer jacket, runs up to them. He hands Barnes a message, and he reads it aloud:

"To all Space Vessels:
Orders from Federation Command:
F.F.S. Baruna *taken by mutineers. Commence full-scale search. Scan all habitable planets within ten parsecs of Earth."*

"We're only six and a half parsecs from Earth," Mumford says. "They'll be able to track us here!"

Turn to page 109.

Three months have passed since the *Baruna* landed on Alpha. In that time you've had good luck and bad luck. The good luck has been that in the forays from base camp you've found edible plants—nutlike berries growing in the midst of little tufted plants. The berries taste rather like bitter chocolate. At first you and the others were unwilling to try them. But Barnes ordered Fenton to taste them, with no ill effect, and now they've become one of your basic food sources.

Even more exciting, you've come upon herds of quadrapeds that look like caribou. Barnes and Kronick have taken to hunting these creatures— dohkoes, as Mumford has named them—with their laser pistols and have had no trouble providing enough meat to eat and hides to wear for everyone.

The bad luck is that the dohkoes have become much shier and now run from the sight of humans. Now you have to track them farther and farther away from base camp. And since Barnes, Kronick, and Fenton have been wasteful in the use of their laser pistols, their power packs are almost exhausted, and there's no way to recharge them.

Turn to page 32.

The *Baruna* coasts toward planet Alpha, retro-engines firing. There's an air of tense expectancy aboard the ship.

The planet is now visible through the forward view ports. The computer-enhanced images on the control room display screens give more information than one could obtain even by looking through a powerful telescope. But there's something about looking at an object with your own eyes that gives you a feel for a place that electronic images fail to convey. You leave the console and move to one of the view ports. As the planetary disc grows larger you can see the planet quite clearly. Polar ice caps extend almost halfway to the planet's equator, but you also see patches of greenish brown and patches of blue. Cloud cover is about fifty percent. You feel a flush of joy and excitement—Alpha is a live planet. You and the other crew members have a chance.

You dash back to the control room and find the others equally excited. Atmosphere scan shows twenty percent oxygen, seventy-five percent nitrogen, two percent carbon dioxide, and no toxic gases—almost the same mix as on Earth!

A few minutes later, the planet looms up so large before you that you get that sudden change of orientation so familiar to space travelers—instead of heading toward a planet in space, you're diving down to it!

"Cross-thrusters—point seven," Barnes commands. "We'll orbit a few times to pick out a landing site."

Turn to page 73.

"I'll have no part in this business," you say loudly to make sure Captain Tyler hears you. Your voice quivers nonetheless, because you're afraid Jack Barnes will make you get in the shuttle, or simply eject you into cold black space.

You're almost relieved when he angrily shoves you aside. "You'll regret this, yellow belly!"

He closes and seals the hatch himself. The *Baruna* shudders, and you hear a muffled roar as the shuttle is jettisoned into space.

"Your punishment will come later," Barnes says. "I want you to worry about it. *Full speed to Genthe*," he calls out.

Barnes assigns work stations to everyone. He orders you to stand watch by the communications monitors.

Turn to page 12.

You're more curious about the charras than afraid of them; they certainly don't look dangerous. And you're afraid that if you tell Barnes about them he'll kill them for their fur and meat—he'll just think of them as *supplies!*

You take the little charra in your arms and wade across the stream. Others—adults and young ones—chirp and whistle in a way that is not like human speech, and yet is much more varied than animal sounds. One female, who seems to be the mother of the young one you're holding, comes forward and takes it from you.

"Chk, chk," another says to you, followed by a rapid series of chirps.

You watch the others talking among themselves. They gesture a lot with their furry arms, so you start gesturing, too.

The charras are delighted. They are such good mimes that you're soon able to understand most of what they're saying by watching their signs and gestures. You learn that they feed on succulent plants that grow along riverbanks. (They offer you some of their food and it's very tasty.) You also learn that the weather will soon get much colder. And in fact the charras are leaving at dawn the next day for their winter grounds. They invite you to sleep overnight in their cave on a soft bed of grass and then come with them on their journey.

Turn to page 35.

You tell Barnes about Katar, and he accepts your recommendation to set a course for the planet.

During the long trip, the other crew members, except for Mumford, become even more quarrelsome. And Barnes is the worst. You wonder what will happen when you reach Katar. It doesn't seem likely that Fenton and Kronick will put up with Barnes's dictatorial ways once they're off the ship.

As the ship approaches it, the star Polaris becomes brighter and brighter until it's the most dazzling star in the sky. Spirits rise, and Barnes and the others talk about how they will forge a new empire on Katar.

Eagerly you scan for a sign of the planet, but its image is lost in the glare of the mother star. At last you spot Katar, but you're not cheered by its reddishbrown color. Soon, computer telemetry confirms your worst fears. The star Polaris is much brighter and hotter than the Earth's sun. As a result, Katar is much too hot to support life. Even at the poles the temperature is above the boiling point!

There can be no refuge on this planet, and there's not enough fuel to reach any other.

The End

As you talk, clouds move across the horizon. Soon rain begins to fall. The desert sands soak it up immediately, turning a darker yellow because of the moisture.

"Come. We will go to our village," Catharine Maslow says.

She and the others lead you some three miles away from the desert to a hilly, green area. The land is cultivated, and orchards ring the valley. Old-fashioned but comfortable-looking houses dot the slopes of the valley. At the center of this community more houses are arranged in a circle around a large green. A wooden frame meeting house stands at one end. Simple, elegant, clean.

"You can live here with us, not that you have much choice," Catharine Maslow says. "Almost no one comes here; and, of course, we never leave, nor do we want to. As I said, you are welcome."

You look at Walker, Nan Pacella, Captain Tyler. Then you look at Catharine Maslow and her followers. Unless you're rescued some day, this will be your world.

The End

A black look crosses Barnes's face. "They've spotted us already, even though we're still six million miles away!"

"It's those new high-intensity sensors," Kronick says.

Barnes passes his fingers nervously through his hair. "Acknowledge the message, Kronick. We don't want them to think something's wrong."

Turn to page 80.

"Let's go, Captain," you say. "We don't have too many choices or chances. The shuttle's running low on both fuel and food. And we can't just drift about forever."

"Okay. My old charts show two planets that might be inhabited. The smaller of the two is Dompuss. The larger and more interesting of the two is a planet called Kali." The captain peers over Nan Pacella's shoulder at her computer display of charts for the Shiva system.

Kali. . . . That name sounds familiar. Where have you heard it mentioned before? you wonder.

"Not much information on either planet," Nan says. "So, let's proceed with caution."

Walker, as usual, is nervously fidgeting with a microcomputer, entering and clearing data. You make a mental note not to rely on him if serious trouble develops.

"Entry permit in full effect. We will be following a laser guide," Nan says.

The shuttle locks onto the laser beam and is moved like a toy on a string through space. The ride becomes bumpy as the shuttle leaves space and sinks into the atmosphere.

Turn to page 55.

When you return to the base camp, you find Barnes, Kronick, and Fenton sitting on a rock, speaking in low tones.

"Where's Mumford?" you ask.

Barnes stands up and steps very close to you, as if to remind you that he's bigger and stronger than you are. "We sent him off with his backpack—to find a new home." He glares at you. "We had a disagreement and he challenged my authority."

You're shocked. Mumford was your only friend in this unsavory crowd. "New home?—on this planet!" you shout angrily.

Barnes seizes your shoulder in a viselike grip. "This planet is our spaceship now, and I'm the captain! What I say goes, or else you'll get the same treatment Mumford got!"

You'd leave the others for good and set out after the charras, but you have no supplies. And Barnes isn't about to give you any to go off on your own. So you tell the others of your discovery of the charras.

"These creatures . . ." Barnes says, an evil gleam in his eye, "they're made of meat, aren't they? They could supply our food over the winter."

"We can't eat the charras," you say. "They're too much like people—"

Barnes turns on you, fury in his eyes. "We'll hunt what I say we hunt."

Turn to page 38.

"Hide in the hills!" Barnes sneers, his face grim. He obviously doesn't think much of your idea. But apparently he can't think of anything better. He nods. "Okay, we'll land on the equatorial plain— longitude one hundred fifty-five degrees east."

During the next six hours the *Baruna* arcs smoothly around the planet, glides through the troposphere, and sets down on a grassy plain near a lush tropical forest.

"There's lots of food to live off in that forest," Barnes says hopefully.

"Won't they track us down?" Fenton asks.

"They won't even look for us," Barnes snaps. "I've rigged the ship to blow up. It'll look as if it crashed and exploded. The ship will be practically vaporized, and they'll think we were, too."

"That might be a good idea," you say, as you point up toward the sky, "but what about *that!*" You've spotted two armed shuttle craft approaching from the east.

"How'd they get here so fast?" Barnes groans as he watches the craft zeroing in on you, so close you can see the name *Medea* on each of their hulls. There's no story you can make up now— you're certain to be tried, convicted, and punished as mutineers.

The End

As you're sitting on a rock at base camp wondering what you can do about the situation, you're distracted by Fenton and Barnes arguing with each other.

"Don't worry, Barnes," Fenton shouts. "I won't waste all my laser power. I'm saving one blast for the right moment!"

Barnes doesn't say anything. He just smiles at Fenton and runs his finger over the scar on his face.

Did Fenton mean he would save a laser charge to use on Barnes? You guess that Barnes won't wait to see if Fenton is planning to do him in. He'll strike first when he gets the chance.

Turn to page 77.

You look at Nan quickly. Has she gone mad, too? you wonder. Then you see what she's staring at—a blip on the communicator screen. And it's growing larger as it draws nearer the shuttle.

"Can you tell what it is?" you ask.

The captain, too, has been studying the data on the screen. "It's a Federation Explorer," he says. "It must be coming to investigate the disappearance of the *Baruna*. It looks like we'll make it home after all."

But not too soon, you silently hope. You've always wanted to roam around space in a Federation Explorer.

The End

"And how do I explain the message Kronick sent out signed by Tyler?" Barnes asks in a hard voice.

"You say you wanted to tell the Admiral personally," you say.

"Okay," says Barnes, "I guess that's the only thing to do."

As the *Baruna* sets down at base Alpha, only a few hundred meters from the Federation battle cruiser *Medea,* you wonder why Barnes agreed so easily. It would be more in keeping with his character to try something desperate.

"This is Admiral Mathis of the *Medea,*" the radio speaker announces. "Welcome to Genthe. We will come aboard to greet you, Captain Tyler, as soon as your ship is docked."

"Thank you, sir," Barnes radios back.

What is Barnes up to? you wonder. You're determined not to go along with him further if you can help it.

The moment the ship docks, Barnes turns around and faces you and the others. His eyes have that same crazed look you saw in them when he forced Captain Tyler into the shuttle craft. But there's no time for him to speak. A loud rap sounds on the main hatch.

"Open it," Barnes tells Kronick, who quickly activates the mechanism.

Turn to page 84.

The next morning you go with the charras on their trek. They carry their supply of nuts and fruits in animal hides which they sling over their backs and tie around their shoulders, leaving their arms free. Occasionally, as you hike across the plains, you see lionlike creatures or a herd of dohkoes, on which the lions prey. Except for large soaring birds, which remind you of vultures, there are few other signs of life. The smaller creatures have already migrated.

That night, under the open sky, you hear the throaty sounds of the lions crouched in the grass nearby. You can't understand why they don't attack the charras, who carry no weapons. Perhaps the charras are not good to eat, you think, recalling how on Earth, certain species of plants and insects protect themselves simply by tasting bad. Maybe it's *your* scent that has attracted the lions.

Turn to page 42.

Two days later you and the tribe of charras reach a warmer region, which you call the peat lands. Though you've been traveling north and the huge, dull sun hangs so low above the horizon that you can feel no warmth from it at all, you feel heat coming up from the dark spongy land. The flora is as lush as you'd expect to find in a tropical rain forest. Huge feathery trees send their spires toward the sky.

You and the charras camp near a beautiful cascade of water that looks almost rose-colored in the deep red light of the sun. By now you've begun to understand some of the chirps and whistles that the charras use to communicate, and they have begun to understand some of the words you speak, which to them must sound equally strange. You understand that you have reached their winter grounds, and that the rest of the planet will soon be raked by icy winds. Only the peat lands—sheltered by a ridge of mountains and warmed by the heat rising through the ground—are habitable in winter.

During Alpha's winter you learn the language and ways of the charras and become an adopted member of their tribe. You play and hunt and forage with them. You make friends as close as any you've ever had. After a while you feel as if you've always been one of them—as if you've lived two completely separate lives.

The End

All the laser packs have been used up. Now you and the others have only your camping gear and a few simple tools and knives. In the course of a few days your technological level has been set back from being one of the most advanced in the galaxy to that of primitive dwellers on the planet Earth.

"We must go out on the plains and hunt," Barnes says.

You and the others make spears by lashing knives to the rods used for propping up your tent. You sharpen rocks and bind them to stout sticks to make axes. As you're making hunting weapons, a chill wind springs up. The temperature drops below freezing for the first time. Winter has arrived.

The next day the four of you—neophyte hunters—set forth across the steppes. About midday you spot a herd of dohkoes, and begin to track them, but your chances look bleak. Fenton and Kronick are always bickering—making much too much noise, and it doesn't help when Barnes yells at them to stop. Alerted to danger, the dohkoes race across the plains. You know you'll never catch them.

Turn to page 112.

The first dull, brownish light is beginning to fill the sky, when you're awakened by a terrifying noise—the deafening roar of a lion almost on top of you! Then, a bloodcurdling scream—Kronick's!

Suddenly the tent collapses, and everything is a tangle of bodies and gear and shredded nylon cloth. You roll away and manage to wriggle through the debris and get to your feet. Then all is silent and still.

You stand looking at the scene before you: Kronick is dead, horribly mauled by a lion. In a bloody tangle of tent cloth the lion itself lies dead, Barnes's spear thrust deep into its chest. Barnes stands nearby, looking at you as if he doesn't see you. His eyes are glazed over. You feel yourself shaking: you're alone with this killer of men and lions, with no tent and no supplies.

Exchanging hardly more than a word or two, you and Barnes bury Kronick and then cook lion meat, for you must eat something if you're to survive another day's hike across the plains.

Turn to page 58.

By the afternoon of the second day of your trek, tempers are shorter than ever. But you catch sight of another herd of dohkoes. Barnes decides on a plan. He, Kronick, and Fenton will circle around and take up positions on the other side of the herd. You are to wait until they're in position and then charge the animals.

As soon as everyone is set, you run toward the dohkoes, yelling as loud as you can. They stampede, veering in Fenton's direction. But instead of spearing one, he panics and runs for safety—straight toward Barnes! Furious, Barnes throws his spear at the closest dohkoe as it runs past, but the spear goes wild. It strikes Fenton square in the chest, knocking him flat. As the dohkoes gallop across the plain, you and Kronick run to the fallen man.

Turn to page 69.

The next afternoon, while the group takes a noonday rest, a young male charra, smaller than the one you rescued from the stream, becomes fascinated with a flower sticking up above the tall grass. You watch him run toward it, eager to pick it. The other charras are distracted, looking toward the distant hills.

It occurs to you that the young one has gone too far, and you imitate the chirping sound the charras use as a signal. Several adults, now seeing how far the young one has wandered, let forth a shrill whistle. The little charra stops in his tracks and turns toward the group. Even at this distance you can see the guilty look on his face.

Suddenly a lion charges! The adults whistle frantically, and the young charra starts running toward safety, but the lion is much faster than he is.

Turn to page 83.

"Five . . . four . . . three . . . two . . . one, go!" comes the emotional command from the captain.

With a rumble, the shuttle breaks off from the spacecraft, and flies into space.

"Direction, please, Captain?" Nan Pacella asks calmly, even though she, too, must know you have little hope of survival no matter which course the captain sets.

Suddenly, Captain Tyler is overcome with a violent seizure. His eyes roll back, his body jerks in muscular spasms. He's incapable of control. Nan rushes to his aid, while Walker tries to control the flight of the shuttle. Someone has to make a decision, and since no one is doing it, you take command of the shuttle.

If you choose to follow the Baruna, *with the hope of getting on board and overthrowing Barnes, turn to page 50.*

If you choose to set course for the quarantined system Barnes mentioned, turn to page 56.

Barnes hurls his spear, and then lets out a whoop of delight as it slashes through the young animal's back. But suddenly he's surrounded by charras. They move with such speed that all you see is Barnes looking out at them one moment and lying dead the next.

The charras turn toward you. You wonder whether they will spare you. After all, you weren't the one who killed their young one. Then you see the expression in their eyes: They know you *could* have tried to save the little one, but you didn't. You're as guilty as Barnes, and soon meet the same fate as he.

The End

"The usual boring Federation reports," you mumble to yourself, scanning the scrolling computer screen.

A moment later your boredom disappears as you read a message for the *Baruna:*

> To F.F.S. Baruna, *Captain Philip Tyler:*
> *The Federation battle cruiser* Medea *will be in Genthe while you are there. You will report to Admiral Mathis for instructions after docking.*
> *Signed/Fleet Command.*

Not good news for the mutineers, you think. They had assumed there would be no Federation military presence on Genthe and that they could do whatever they liked on that primitive planet. Now they'll have to face a fleet admiral, whose first question will be, "Where is Captain Tyler?"

Go on to the next page.

You're tempted to erase the information from the computer. If Jack Barnes learns of the Federation presence, he won't dare to land on Genthe. His recourse will no doubt be to set out for the distant Ceres star system, with only a fair chance of reaching it, and no assurance of finding a habitable planet.

But if you don't tell Barnes about the message, and he lands on Genthe, you're liable to be hanged with the others as a mutineer.

If you bring the message to Jack Barnes's attention, turn to page 6.

If you try to erase the communication from the computer's memory, turn to page 3.

You pick up a rock and hurl it—the rock lands well short of the young charra but achieves the effect you desired. The charra scampers toward the woods. Barnes hurls his spear too late.

In a rage he rushes you.

You turn to run, though you don't doubt he'll catch you. But suddenly, streaks of blue fur are on either side of Barnes. Faster than your eye can follow, he's on the ground with two charras standing over him!

You watch in awe as Barnes lies begging for mercy. These creatures, which look so harmless, have a weapon unknown on earth—the ability to move with such tremendous speed they can dispatch their prey in a flash of light. The charras stand chirping and whistling to each other. You can't understand what they're saying, but it's soon obvious they're having an argument. One of them points to Barnes, still cringing on the ground, and then points to you. Suddenly you guess what the creature is saying: "They're too much like us to eat!"

You hope the charra pointing at you wins the argument.

The End

"We'll shadow the *Baruna*," you tell Walker. "There's a blind spot behind the aft cargo loading bay. See that hump? We can drift back to there, turn off our energy supply, and be sucked along by the *Baruna*'s gravitational field."

"No!" Walker shouts. "They'll see us. Barnes is crazy. They'll kill us!"

"Calm down, Walker. It's worth a try. Nan, do you agree?" you ask.

"Yes, I do," Nan says, making the captain as comfortable as possible.

Moments later, your shuttle craft slides into place behind the *Baruna*. Suddenly, you realize that the *Baruna* is moving in a direction that surprises you. The ship is headed back to Earth!

"I wonder what their game is?" you muse.

"Barnes once said something about holding Earth hostage," Walker says. "He mentioned it as a possibility by a terrorist group. Maybe he was talking out loud about his own plans."

"Did he say how he would do it?" you ask.

"Well, he did say neurotoxins would be easy to spread and sure to kill."

"They occupy so little space, he could have smuggled a crate aboard with enough neurotoxins in solution to ruin civilization on Earth," the captain says, sitting up and shaking his head.

Go on to the next page.

"I think you've hit on it," says Nan. "He's always been too much for me. Too sincere. Too good to be true."

"And quite mad," the captain adds.

"We've got to stop him," you shout.

"Well, we either try to stop him and the *Baruna* now, or we alert Earth and have them intercept him before the *Baruna* enters the Transit Zone," Nan reasons out loud.

You wonder if you could slip unnoticed into the *Baruna* through the cargo bay. The mutineers probably aren't expecting you to reenter the spaceship.

Sending a message to Earth warning the space patrol of Barnes's plan is less risky, but the *Baruna* might intercept and block your transmission. The captain looks at you, waiting for your decision.

If you decide to enter the Baruna *through the cargo bay, turn to page 65.*

If you try to warn Earth, turn to page 94.

Barnes is so worked up that no one is going to argue with him. "Return to stations!" he orders. "Mumford! Plot a course to Ceres—hyperdrive two point five."

Once the ship has attained interstellar speed, Barnes orders you to man the planetary radiation monitor.

"Mumford should have gone with Tyler," he mutters. "I want you to run the programs designed to detect undiscovered planets on the way to Ceres."

"Yes, sir," you reply, though you don't have much hope of finding any planets, and if you do they're not likely to be habitable. You shake your head as you think about the predicament you're all in. And having Barnes in command isn't any help. He's even more reckless and compulsive than Captain Tyler was.

Turn to page 10.

"Wake up! Wake up!" Nan shouts. "We're approaching the Shiva system, and I'm receiving strange signals."

"What kind of signals?" you ask.

"Radio signals. But I've never seen a pattern like it before. My computer rejects the input and signals overload."

"Any rhythm to the signals?" Captain Tyler asks. He seems alert and interested for the first time since his seizure.

"Yes. Classic repeat of audio signal. Wavelength could be one over F," Nan replies.

The captain perks up. "Signal back," he says. "Signal back using this code."

The captain pulls an old, leather notebook from an inside pocket.

"The signal is C-H-O-M-O-L-U-N-G-M-A"— the captain spells the word slowly to Nan—"it's a symbol code that might still be recognized by some groups in this system."

Nan taps the code into the computer and then hits the transmit key.

Turn to page 64.

"Looks like we're headed for Kali. Prepare for landing," says Nan confidently.

Thunk!

The shuttle lands shakily on a small rocket-launch-and-recovery pad. Lights flicker on the perimeter of the pad, and the shuttle is bathed in a sickly blue glow. A voice penetrates the silence.

"Leave all weapons on board. Descend, captain first. Place your hands out in front of you. Do not speak unless spoken to."

"You could remain hidden in the shuttle with a blaster ready," the captain says to you. "Then, if we need help, I'll signal you. How about it?"

If you agree to hide on the shuttle, turn to page 78.

If you decide to go out with the others, turn to page 74.

As you head the shuttle craft away from the course of the *Baruna,* you say, "Nan, that quarantined system Barnes mentioned, what's it called?"

"Shiva system," she says, helping the captain to a seat.

Shiva. You recall having read reports of an illness or plague in the Shiva system. But there were other suggestions: that Shiva is a secret Federation base; that it's a prison colony for other solar systems. But all the reports were based on rumor. Only the top command of the Federation knows the real truth about Shiva.

"What else do you know about the system, Nan?"

"It's in a strange corner of this galaxy, surrounded by huge gas clouds and an array of black holes," she says.

"How long has it been quarantined?"

"Every star chart I've ever seen, and some of those charts go back eleven hundred years, has Shiva system marked 'Quarantined—Do Not Enter,'" Nan answers.

Go on to the next page.

"Well, it's our only hope—we don't have much fuel left. What kind of ETA can you give us?" you ask.

"ETA . . . twelve space days," Nan says, punching data into the shuttle computer, "assuming all goes well and we don't meet meteor showers or hostile pirate craft."

The captain is beginning to recover from his seizure. He sits up, blinks his eyes, and asks, "What happened? Where am I?" You reassure him that all is well. Still somewhat dazed, he nods, and you continue in command of the shuttle craft.

Turn to page 67.

With spears and axes in hand, you and Barnes trudge silently across the tundra. The temperature has sunk well below freezing, and there's no sign of life in any direction. Neither of you were able to eat more than a few bites of gristly, foul tasting lion meat; and you can feel your strength waning away. You'll have no shelter from the cold tonight. Either you'll freeze, or the lions will get you, or you'll be too weak to walk. It already seems that your fate is sealed.

You glance at the enormous dull sun hanging low in the western sky. An hour more and the top of the sun will set, then darkness will swiftly follow.

"Look up ahead!" Barnes's excitement comes through his dry, husky voice.

You had already seen what he's pointing toward, but had thought it was a low bank of clouds. Now you see trees—a forest! You quicken your pace, feeling as if you've seen an oasis in the desert.

Turn to page 79.

One day while you're sharing the watch with Mumford, he looks up from his console. "Say, take a look at this."

You glance at coordinates showing on the screen.

"Your scanners showed nothing there—in the Libra sector?" he asks.

You shake your head. "Nothing luminous. What's your data?"

Mumford glances out the view port at the star-studded black space. "Our course has been very slightly affected by a gravity aberration bearing point zero two over zero seven seven. We'll be abreast of whatever it is within a few hours. It's very close."

"Yet we can't get it on the scanners," you observe. "Could it be—?"

"Right," Mumford interrupts. "A brown dwarf star—just below fusion point, and there's an aberration in the plot line indicating one or more planets, very close in."

"We'd better tell Barnes," you say.

Turn to page 68.

Moments later you hear a rustling noise behind you, and you turn quickly.

No one. Nothing.

You go on.

Again, you hear a noise.

You signal for silence.

"Captain, did you hear that?" you ask.

Before he can answer, you're surrounded by a band of people. They look like normal humans, despite being dressed in old-fashioned clothes. You've seen pictures of such clothes in the history tapes in the computer library back at space school. They were the clothes people on Earth wore back in the 1980s and into the early part of the twenty-first century. Strange. Strange indeed, you think.

"Welcome to Dompuss. Put down your weapons. We mean you no harm," says a tall, elderly woman. "Please follow us."

"Thank you for your welcome," the captain replies. "We will follow you."

You hang back. You're not entirely convinced that these people are friendly. The captain could be making a mistake.

If you follow the captain, turn to page 95.

If you try to dash back to the shuttle, turn to page 98.

As the ship is buffeted by ion particles, the crew gropes for something to hold to.

Then, almost as quickly as it started, the ion storm passes.

"We're out of the storm," Mumford reports from the control center.

"Very well," Captain Tyler says, as if nothing out of the ordinary had happened. Not even a flicker of a smile crosses his face. The crew watches silently as he leaves the bridge to return to his quarters.

A half hour later, Mumford calls the captain out of his quarters. "Another ion storm, dead ahead, Captain," he reports as the captain joins him on the bridge. "It looks even stronger than the last one."

"Very well," the captain replies in a monotone. "We'll ride it out."

"We may not be so lucky this time, Captain," Barnes says.

You begin to shiver. Captain Tyler is a capable space pilot, but he's so unwilling to compromise.

Suddenly Barnes is standing on the bridge, a laser pistol in his hand. Kronick and Mumford are standing behind him.

"Raise your hands and get back against the bulkhead!" Barnes cries, pointing his gun at the captain's back. "I'm taking over this ship!"

Turn to page 105.

The four of you wait. Minutes slip by. The monitor becomes silent, and the OVERLOAD signal on the computer screen disappears.

"Patience, crew," the captain says. He seems to have recovered fully and, although shaky, is back in control.

"I don't like this," Walker says, jumping up and pacing about the small compartment.

A series of beeps from the computer startles the four of you.

"What is it, Nan?" you ask.

Nan's fingers tap quickly over the keyboard. A message appears on the monitor. "Why, it's an old-fashioned entry-permit code used to guard colonies years ago," she says. "I've read about them, but I've never seen one in use."

"That's what I thought," the captain says. "But, once we accept the entry permit, we're locked in for a ride to their colony—assuming, of course, that there still is one."

"What do you mean?" you ask.

"Only that life-forms might be gone and we're dealing with a still-functioning computer guard system. Again, my young friend, I ask you to choose. Your young life is as valuable as my own. Do we go, or get out now?"

If you decide to go ahead into this unknown territory, turn to page 28.

If you decide to back out, turn to page 70.

"I'm going into the *Baruna*," you say. "We've got to stop Barnes now. He's a threat to the entire universe!"

"I'll go with you," Nan says.

Captain Tyler starts to protest, but you convince him your plan is best.

"This is our only chance to stop Barnes," you explain. "If his plan is to hold Earth hostage—it's now or never."

Walker brings the shuttle close to the cargo bay and maneuvers it into the docking port. There's a *thunk* as the shuttle locks into the mother ship.

Captain Tyler tries to stand and help you open the hatch, but he slumps back into his chair, still weak from his seizure.

"Good luck," Walker mumbles as he busies himself with the computer.

Your hands fumble with the hatch, but finally it opens into the air lock in the cargo area.

"Okay. We're in," you tell Tyler and Walker through your throat microphone. "Back off for now. We'll signal when we're ready to return."

Fortunately, there's no one in the cargo receiving area, but you have a strong feeling that you're being watched. You look around in silence, breathing the stuffy air. Dark bays loaded with crates and barrels fill the cargo space.

"Who's there?" comes a sharp growl.

Turn to page 89.

TRASH EVACUATOR

Moments later, Walker taps you on the shoulder. "Look what I found," he says, holding up a vial marked NEUROTOXINS. EXTREME DANGER. "It has a timed perforator top. Fortunately, the top's still holding."

"Jettison it!" you command. "Quick!"

Walker places the vial in the trash evacuator and with a *whoosh*, it's sucked out into the vacuum of space.

You wonder if Barnes planted that vial on board the shuttle.

You continue to run the small craft as efficiently as possible. The captain is recovering, and you realize that his reputation could well have come about as a result of his medical problem, which he'd managed to keep hidden until his voyage.

Hours later, after the ship is safely on its way toward the Shiva system, you close your eyes. You're exhausted, and soon you're asleep.

Turn to page 53.

A few minutes later the entire crew is gathered in the control room. While Mumford is describing his finding to Barnes, you pick up infrared emanations and feed the telemetry into the computer.

"Well?" Barnes demands.

You study the data display on your screen. "There is a planet about two million miles from the dwarf star," you announce. "The planet is almost Earth's size, so there should be enough atmosphere."

"Let's land there," Tim Fenton cries. "The Federation police will never find us."

"They'll never find us if we're baked to death, or frozen to death," Barnes says sarcastically. "Well?" He looks into your eyes. "Shall we try this planet?"

"If we do, and it doesn't work out, we won't have enough fuel to reach Ceres," Mumford mumbles.

If you recommend going to the planet of the brown dwarf star, turn to page 11.

If you recommend continuing on to Ceres, turn to page 15.

Kronick arrives first. He carefully removes the spear from Fenton's chest, and tries to stop the flow of blood. Finally, he realizes his efforts are useless. He looks up gravely at you and Barnes. "He's dead."

No one says anything. You, Kronick, and Barnes use your spears to dig a hole to bury Fenton, then you silently continue across the plain, knowing your chances are worse now that there are only three of you.

The afternoon brings no good luck, and that night you again huddle in the tent. You hear the lions outside, but this time you're too exhausted to stay awake. You're soon sleeping soundly, sometimes having good dreams about food, sometimes bad dreams about lions.

Turn to page 39.

"Let's get out, Captain," you say. "I agree with Walker. I don't like this, either. It seems too simple, too easy, like a trap."

Nan nods in agreement, and she and Walker make the necessary adjustments to head the ship away from this unknown zone.

The computer flashes a warning: YOU MUST NOT LEAVE. IF YOU LEAVE WE ARE DOOMED. The message repeats continuously.

You stare at the monitor. You feel as if the message is aimed at you personally.

"Its like a siren song," the captain says. "Many thousands of years ago, a Greek warrior was lured to his death by sirens. This is a different lure, but it could have the same effect. We must be strong."

"I'm not sure that this entry permit is for the main Shiva system, anyway," Nan says as she reviews the data on the monitor. "It could be coming from a renegade outpost."

There is a small, one-person space pod aboard the shuttle for rapid penetration of danger zones. Its range is about that needed for a flyby of the zone below.

You must decide what to do right away.

If you give in to the siren song and decide to use the space pod, turn to page 86.

If you reject the siren song, turn to page 82.

"Relax!" Mumford says sharply. "It's giving off plenty of infrared radiation. We'll see it soon."

Even as he speaks, the dull red disc of the dwarf star becomes visible. It looks like the sun seen through a heavy haze.

Barnes still seems nervous. You're nervous, too. You never know when his fear will change to anger. Suddenly his face lights up. "I see a planet!"

"And another!" Mumford says.

Sure enough, you can see two tiny discs on the display screen.

"Which one is for us?" Barnes asks.

"The dwarf star's surface temperature is only two thousand degrees," Mumford says.

"Not much hotter than Venus," Barnes mutters.

"This star wasn't hot enough to ignite," says Mumford. "It's like a huge, glowing ember."

"We definitely should go to the inner planet," you say.

"It's small. It may not have enough atmosphere," Mumford says, looking at you.

"We'd freeze on the outer planet," you say.

Hearing this, Barnes orders the slight course adjustment necessary to land on the inner planet.

"For better or worse, it's going to be our home," he says. "Planet Alpha, we'll name it."

"Fire braking-thrusters as necessary," he orders. "We'll orbit this little world a few times before attempting a landing."

Turn to page 21.

For the next hour you're too busy monitoring data to talk to anyone—you're just part of the machinery. Then, Barnes gives the command to land on a broad plain near the equator. The ground here is covered only with short tufted grass and tundra. Gravity is .86. All conditions are well within the *Baruna*'s capabilities, and the ship sets down as smoothly as a bird.

A cheer goes up, and a few minutes later you're all standing outside. A brisk wind is blowing from the north. The huge brownish red sun—only two million miles away—looking ten times as big as the sun on Earth, is almost directly overhead.

"I guess this is the warmest it gets at noon here in the tropics," Mumford observes, shivering a little in the chilly north wind.

Turn to page 18.

"I'm going with you, Captain," you say.

"Okay. But I warn you, this planet and its people might be troublesome. There was talk years ago of renegades and outcasts heading for the Shiva system."

The air outside the shuttle is stifling hot and hard to breathe. The surface of the launchpad is uneven and sticky. It smells like a freshly tarred road.

"Captain, look!" you say, pointing at two large tanks. They're old and rusty.

The captain looks at the tanks and starts to speak, but a sharp crackling sound interrupts him. You dive to the ground just as a beam of light flashes over your head. Another beam hits the ground a few feet away from you and vaporizes a patch of land as you watch.

Lunging to the left, you and the captain dash for the flank of the nearest tank. Nan and Walker stand transfixed in the bluish light, frozen in panic.

There's another sharp crackling sound, and a beam of energy nearly hits Nan and Walker. The lead tank moves forward as the two terrified crew members run back to the space shuttle.

Go on to the next page.

"There's no escape," comes a harsh voice from behind one of the tanks.

"Captain," you whisper, "I've got a blaster."

"Get ready," responds the captain. "But wait until I say to fire."

"No escape," echoes the voice as a man steps out from the shelter of the tank.

He is grotesque. Wisps of hair poke out of his head and his features melt together in a slimy mass.

"Fire!" says the captain.

Turn to page 93.

You decide to take a long walk and see if you can think over what to do. You strap on a day pack and head out across the steppes. After an hour's hike you reach a broad stream. Your heart leaps as you see fish swimming by. You're determined to learn how to catch them. If the dohkoes leave the range, fishing may be essential for survival.

You stifle a gasp when you see faces peering out from the bushes on the other side of the stream. Then a creature steps out from its cover and walks toward the water. Is it humanoid or not? you wonder. It's about half your size and walks upright. Its body is covered with beautiful dark blue fur. It has long arms, like a gorilla, yet its face looks more human than a gorilla's face. You hear one of the creatures calling from the bushes—*"Ukk, chh, klg, chk-chk-chk."* The creature who had approached the stream answers. It points at you. Again, *Chh, chh, klg, chk."* Suddenly the animal—you name its species *charra*—starts wading across the stream straight toward you. At the same time you hear a furious din from the forest. One of the charras comes out—it's much larger than the first, probably its mother. Meanwhile the little one has almost reached you. It's smiling like a happy child—it wants to play!

If you pick up the charra and carry it back to its mother, turn to page 23.

If you decide you'd better get back to base camp and tell the others of your discovery, turn to page 29.

"I'll stay, Captain. They probably won't search the shuttle right away," you say hopefully. "What's the signal for help?"

The captain thinks quickly and answers, "I'll drop my gloves." Then he steps out of the shuttle.

Dropping to the floor of the shuttle, you squirm into the space between the computers and the life-support management systems. Although you've always disliked weapons, you're comforted by the hand-held blaster. You adjust it for STUN rather than LETHAL and settle down to wait and watch through a small view port.

Turn to page 87.

Hope provides the strength you need to reach the bountiful country that lies before you. Before the great sun has half set, you and Barnes are feasting on nuts and fruits in a grassy glade surrounded by tall, rubbery trees.

Then, both of you see it at the same moment—a small, furry two-legged creature peering at you through the trees—a young charra!

"Meat," Barnes calls at you.

He seizes his spear and begins to stalk the creature. It stands innocently watching. You want to protect this humanlike creature; yet you fear Barnes's anger if you cross him.

If you throw something toward the charra to scare it away, turn to page 48.

If you decide to do nothing to stop Barnes, turn to page 45.

Kronick keyboards a message into the computer. It shows up on the monitor as it is being sent.

To Federation battle cruiser Medea *from transport ship* Baruna:
Message received. Will comply. My crew and I look forward to seeing you on Genthe.
Signed: Captain Philip Tyler.

Go on to the next page.

"*You sent that out?* Now they'll expect Tyler to be on board!" Barnes moves as if to smash his fist into Kronick's pale-white face.

You step forward. "Stop! If we fight among ourselves we'll never have a chance."

For once Barnes seems to understand that force isn't the solution to everything. His voice is laden with sarcasm, however, as he jabs a finger almost in your face. "Okay, you're so smart, what would you do?"

If you suggest landing on the other side of the planet and hiding in the hills, turn to page 30.

If you suggest telling Admiral Mathis that Captain Tyler and the others were lost on a mission in the shuttle craft, turn to page 34.

"I guess you're right, Captain, that could be a song of death," you say. "Perhaps we can approach the Shiva system from another quadrant."

"We'll try that," Captain Tyler says, placing his hand on your shoulder. "In space travel as in life," he adds, "you have to learn to distinguish between dangers. Running through a meteor shower, that's just nature at its playful worst. You can judge that. But once you get humanoid intelligence at work, watch out! Anything can—and will—happen."

"Right, Captain," you say. "I'll remember that."

The shuttle craft slowly withdraws until the signal disappears.

Nan Pacella is a superb navigator, and Walker is good at his job of conserving fuel and life support. Soon you're circling the outer rim of the Shiva system searching for a safe entry port. It's like looking for a break in a reef structure surrounding an island.

But finally you see a way in—devoid of major space debris and clear for navigation.

"Computer indicates we're above Dompuss, the second largest of the Shiva system's many planets," Nan reports. "Some signs of life-form. No radio signals, however," she adds.

Turn to page 91.

The nearest adult charra races directly toward the lion. The great tawny animal turns on its small blue attacker. You marvel at the bravery of the charra, about to give up its life to save the baby. Just as the lion as about to close its jaws on its victim, the charra sidesteps with such speed that it seems to move instantaneously. As the lion turns, one of the charra's hands comes down in a lightning stroke on the lion's great head, midway between an eye and an ear. The lion reels as if struck by a rifle shot and staggers away, while the adult charra picks up the young one and returns to the rest of the group.

Turn to page 36.

A moment later Admiral Mathis of the *Medea* walks through the hatch and enters the ship. With him are his chief of staff and two officers. Mathis holds out a hand for Barnes to shake, but his face turns pale when he sees that Barnes has a laser gun trained on him.

"I'm taking you hostage," says Barnes. "I want safe passage to the Albran system."

But Admiral Mathis only laughs. "As a transport officer you haven't kept up with the latest military developments, Barnes. All commanders carry force neutralizers. Your laser gun has no power!"

Turn to page 14.

"Captain, let me do a flyby in the space pod," you say. "I know I thought the entry-permit signal was a trap, but this signal is a cry for help. I just can't leave it alone. I want to check it out."

"It's dangerous," the captain replies.

"It's foolish," Walker says.

"Probably, but I don't care. It's something I have to do," you respond.

The captain nods his agreement.

"Be careful," Nan cautions, as you climb into the torpedo-shaped capsule equipped with radar-enhanced sighting and navigation. There's a clear nose for visual piloting. The pod's life-support package has a time span of about two days. It's hot and uncomfortable inside the cramped space. You have to lie flat on your stomach and direct the pod by adjusting small liquid-nitrogen jets that can turn and even reverse the capsule's direction. But you can't accelerate. There's only one speed.

"Wish me luck. If I'm not back in two days, you're on your own," you say in as cheerful a voice as possible, as the space pod leaves the fragile shelter of the shuttle.

"Good luck," Walker, Nan, and the captain reply in unison.

The pod drifts off in the direction of the entry-permit zone. You concentrate on the dials facing you, ready for any danger.

Turn to page 96.

The captain, Nan, and Walker are about a hundred yards away from the shuttle, walking slowly, with their arms out in front of them. They look awful in the blue light.

The light changes to a bright, clear orange.

The sun is rising. It's morning on Kali. The orb of the sun is blood red.

Now you see that you're in the middle of a vast plain surrounded by low-lying, smooth hills. There are bananalike trees, bamboo groves, and what appear to be rice paddies.

Three large, rusty-looking tanklike vehicles sit at the edge of the launchpad. A figure leans against one of the tanks.

He looks horrible! His face is distorted like a clay figure that has been out in the rain too long. His features melt together in a slimy mass.

"This way, my brave little space voyagers," he says in a venomous voice.

Long netted poles protrude from the turrets on two of the tanks. You watch the turrets begin to swivel with a clack of old, rusted machinery.

"It's a trap!" you yell. But your shout is muffled by the confining spaces of the shuttle cabin.

At that precise moment you see the captain drop his gloves.

Turn to page 111.

You and Nan freeze against a large crate. Seconds tick by, marked by your pounding heartbeat.

"Who's there?" comes the voice again.

Lights flash on!

Men come running.

Sirens pierce the cavernous cargo bay.

You're surrounded, captured, ejected into space.

Spinning crazily, your two bodies drift past the shuttle, where the captain sorrowfully notes in his log the death of two members of his crew.

The End

"We'd better go to Genthe," you tell Barnes. "There's no way we'd make it through the ion storms near Ceres, and we don't have enough fuel to go around them."

"Very well," Barnes says, after checking your sensor reports. He glowers at you as if you were the one responsible for his plight. "But when we land on Genthe, we're sure to be approached by the Federation battle cruiser. Admiral Mathis will want to know what happened to Captain Tyler and the others. What will we say?"

"We could say they went on an inspection mission in the shuttle craft," Fenton offers, "and that it was hit by a meteor."

"He'll never believe that story," Barnes says. "Think of something!" he roars at you.

As the *Baruna* streaks toward Genthe, its fuel supply severely depleted because of course changes, the computer prints a message:

To F.F.S. Baruna *from Federation Command:*
Greetings to Captain Tyler and crew. We have detected your ship en route to Genthe. Direct you to land at base Alpha—next to our ship. We look forward to seeing you.
Signed: Admiral Mathis, Federation Battle Cruiser Medea.

Turn to page 27.

The captain nods and beckons Walker and Nan to go ahead. The shuttle vibrates violently as it enters the system and lands on Dompuss.

The landing site is a sandy mound on the edge of a desert. In the distance you see the sharp, high peaks of a mountain range. They're snow covered. That's a good sign, you think. It means Dompuss has an atmosphere similar to Earth's.

You leave the shuttle, followed by the others. As you suspected, the mobile breathing packs are unnecessary, and you stow them back aboard the shuttle. You carry a weapon, but you feel uncomfortable with it. You hope you won't need to use it.

The air is still. You walk on, heading toward the foothills where you hope to find food.

There's no sign of life, only a feeling in the air—a feeling that something is about to happen.

Turn to page 60.

Two quick blasts from your weapon stun the man.

You run to the stunned figure lying on the ground gurgling. As you reach him, he rises and changes form before your very eyes. He becomes a young man—good-looking, fair-haired, smiling.

"You saved me. You released me from my bondage to the forces of Kali. I salute you," he says.

"We can talk later," you say, "but now let's get back to the shuttle."

Together you dash toward the craft as the tanks start up and rumble off in the opposite direction.

Turn to page 116.

"Let's transmit a warning to Earth," you say. "We'd be outnumbered aboard the *Baruna*."

"But we don't have the transmitter code for verification. It's locked into the *Baruna*'s computer system," Nan says.

"There must be another way," you think aloud. You turn to the captain, hoping for some guidance, but he's preoccupied with a small leather notebook.

"I've got it!" he exclaims, looking up. "I found an emergency transmitter code we used when I was a young apprentice on a transit ship between Mars and Earth. I wrote it down. Here it is."

"Is it still useful?" Walker asks skeptically.

"We won't know until we try," you respond, handing the coded message to Nan.

As Nan starts to transmit the message, you hope the *Baruna* doesn't pick up your signal and block its transmission.

"Faster, Nan. Faster," the captain says, quietly urging her on. Gone is all the harshness he was so infamous for.

Turn to page 108.

Willing to trust the captain's judgment, you hurry forward to join the others. The captain has gained your respect on this voyage, and you're convinced that his reputation for harshness and cruel behavior was never truly earned.

"We are glad to be here," he says, shaking hands with the woman.

You still aren't so sure of that, but you are patient. He continues.

"I sense that I know you—"

"You may know *about* me, Captain, but you weren't born when I and six others exiled ourselves to Dompuss. We did it as a protest to what was happening on Earth," she says. "You probably read about us in school."

"You're Catharine Maslow, aren't you? You were once leader of the World Congress."

"Correct, Captain. As you can see, we have done well. Our original band of seven is now over seven hundred souls. We live in peace, in harmony with this wonderful planet, in hope for others."

"Why is the area quarantined?" you blurt out.

"Simple, my young friend. Ideas are the strongest and most dangerous weapons humans know of. Our ideas about peace and harmony threaten those in power on Earth. We are regarded as extremely dangerous. So Earth leaves us alone, and we leave Earth alone."

Turn to page 26.

Suddenly flashes of light explode in front of your space pod. You feel the nose of the pod shatter, and close your eyes.

You're thrown out of the capsule and tumble in a drifting, floating spasm. You feel as if your body is bursting into a million pieces, like so much dust in a beam of sunlight.

Yet you live. You become a state of consciousness, a spiritual vapor floating through space. You're at home among the stars.

The End

You ease away from the people surrounding you, ready to dash back to the shuttle as soon as you're clear.

Suddenly the elderly woman focuses her gaze on you. You feel trapped inside a telepathic cage.

"We repeat, we mean you no harm. We read minds. We have developed powers of thought, meditation, and mind control. That is what we have done for hundreds of years on this planet. We are the exiles from a dark time in Earth's history. Exiles by desire. Now you have joined us. Welcome," says the woman. "Join us or leave us. But first, listen to us."

You gaze back into the woman's eyes. They're filled with compassion and understanding.

You're suddenly aware—without understanding how you know—that the captain, Nan, and Walker see this woman as you do, and have decided to join the people of Dompuss.

You, too, decide to remain. Immediately the bonds of your telepathic cage loosen, and you are filled with a sense of great joy.

The End

You watch Nan key in the self-destruct code on the communicator. Then the four of you watch the computer screen intently. The blip marking the *Baruna* is still visible. It continues on a path to Earth.

Then it disappears.

"Gone," Nan says quietly.

"Fortunately, the *Baruna* was not in Earth's atmosphere. Earth is safe from the neurotoxins," you say, breathing a sigh of relief. You look at the captain. He seems fully recovered now.

"Well, Captain, you're in command, what do we do now?"

"Head for the nearest habitable planet," he answers. "But I must warn you that we don't have enough food or fuel to reach any habitable planet I know of. Perhaps, with luck—"

"One pinch of luck coming up," Nan says, giggling.

Turn to page 33.

You meet the other crew members, but you have little time to talk to them because everyone is busy with countdown procedures. That night you're only able to catch a few hours sleep. Lift-off is scheduled for five A.M. the next morning.

Your alarm goes off an hour before lift-off. It's still dark when you take your station at the telemetry console.

Despite your lack of sleep, you feel wide awake and tremendously excited to be heading into space. Still, you're a little nervous. You tell yourself that the *Baruna* is a sound ship—as good as most in the fleet—and you know that Tyler is a very experienced captain. But he seems to be a harsh man; and Barnes is a strange character, too. He smiles a lot, but you don't like the way he grins at you—as if he's getting ready to play a mean trick. You wonder what he's really up to.

Suddenly the klaxon warns you to get into your restraints. You listen to the final countdown through your earphones. Moments later, the *Baruna*'s thrusters unleash their fire. The ship lifts off, slowly at first, then gathering speed; it arcs gracefully through the stratosphere and out into the stark blackness of space. Your first space voyage has begun!

Turn to page 4.

Three days pass without incident. Then, just as you've come on duty on the bridge, the ship lurches sharply to starboard. Everyone grabs for a handhold. The display screens are filled with static.

You look anxiously at Captain Tyler. If he's scared, he isn't showing it, you think to yourself.

"It's an ion storm," Mumford says to the captain. "A bad one. I think we should reverse course, sir."

Kronick's panicked voice rushes from the speaker near your head. "Captain, our space drive is being neutralized!"

"Reverse course, captain!" Barnes yells. "Before it's too late!"

But the captain doesn't alter the course. "Get off the bridge, Barnes," the captain orders. "If we shrink from every difficulty, we'll never keep on schedule."

"Very well, sir. I'll go help Kronick in the engine room," Barnes says. As he passes you he whispers, "Get ready to join us."

You have no time to think about what means—the whole ship is vibrating!

Turn to page 62.

"No! We can't do that!" you shout. "There are human lives aboard the *Baruna*. We don't really know if Barnes is out to hold Earth hostage. In fact, the very idea is ridiculous. I can't let you do it." You move quickly to the communicator and switch it off.

"A noble gesture, my friend," the captain says, "but you could be dooming Earth."

"Message from the *Baruna*!" Nan says excitedly. "They're coming to pick us up. Barnes has gone mad, and the crew has overpowered him and is returning the ship to the captain's command."

"What happened?" you ask, anxious for more details.

"Barnes wasn't planning to hold Earth hostage—he was planning to *destroy* Earth by dumping neurotoxins into the atmosphere," Nan replies.

You're glad you didn't allow the captain to destroy the *Baruna*. Now you can continue on your mission in space.

The End

No one answers.

Barnes runs his finger slowly down his scar; his smile grows wider.

"Blast it then!" the captain thunders. "The videos will be locked up for the rest of the trip. And next time something like this happens, each of you will regret it to your dying day!"

He storms out of the wardroom.

"The captain is half crazy," Barnes says.

"If we ever reach Genthe, I'm jumping ship, before the captain goes all-the-way crazy!" Tim Fenton exclaims.

"Pipe down, the captain will hear you," you say.

Fenton jerks his head around at you. "Keep your mouth shut!"

"Everyone back to your stations," Barnes orders. "When the time comes to deal with the captain, I'll be in charge."

Turn to page 101.

Captain Tyler faces Barnes. "What the devil!"

Barnes steps closer, menacing the captain with his gun.

"This is *mutiny*!" the captain shouts. "You'll never get away with it. You'll hang for this, Barnes!"

Jack Barnes merely laughs. "You should thank me for being kindhearted, Captain. I'm going to let you—and anyone who wants to go along—take the shuttle craft. Now move!"

Captain Tyler glares at Barnes. "The nearest habitable planet is half a trillion miles away—and you expect me to get there in a shuttle craft?"

"I'm giving you a chance," Barnes says, then he grins maliciously. "There's a quarantined system a lot closer. You *could* head for that. Now—"

The captain makes a move as if to rush Barnes, then shrinks back when a sizzling beam of laser light flashes past his head, setting off a shower of sparks as it strikes the bulkhead behind him.

"Now!" Barnes yells. His eyes are wide and there is a hint of madness in them.

Turn to page 113.

You follow Nan Pacella into the shuttle. The captain is about to enter the craft behind you, when he stops and faces the mutineers. He shakes his fist and speaks. "Mutineers are a plague to all life-forms in space. They are outcasts. You are choosing a path with *no return.*"

With these ominous words, the captain takes leave of his spaceship and enters the shuttle. The hatch closes with a metallic click, and the lights on the control panel flash Ready For Departure in an electric orange hue.

"All ready, sir," Walker says, in a voice that shows he's fighting to control his rising panic.

"Prepare for takeoff," Captain Tyler shouts.

You notice that *his* voice is nearly out of control.

Turn to page 43.

"Oh, no!" Nan groans. "The signal's reaching Earth, but they're rejecting it. They say we're using an improper transmittal code."

"What now, Captain?" you ask.

"There's one other thing we can try," the captain says, referring again to his small leather notebook. "We'll use the self-destruct code for the *Baruna*. It's always been the captain's option in case of extreme danger from aliens. Barnes can't stop it; he doesn't know about it. Only commanders are given the self-destruct code."

For a moment you waver. Should you allow the captain to carry out this act of destruction? You could turn off the communicator and let the authorities on Earth take care of Barnes, you think.

If you decide to block transmission of the self-destruct code, turn to page 103.

If you decide to take no action, turn to page 99.

"Well," says Barnes, "we'll have to blow up the ship."

"You're crazy," Fenton snaps, but is silenced by Mumford's upraised hand.

"Barnes is right," Mumford says. "Their scans will detect the ship if we leave it intact."

There's a short, heated argument, but the force of logic prevails. Within the hour you and the others have off-loaded all the supplies you can carry and have set up a temporary shelter behind a rock outcropping half a mile away. With a radio signal, Barnes activates a detonator. You hold your ears as a quarter kiloton charge disintegrates the *Baruna*.

Turn to page 19.

You open the view port and fire the blaster three times.

But it's too late. Troops are already storming the shuttle, and you're captured.

Moments later you join the captain, Walker, and Nan in a net suspended from the turret poles of the two tanks, swinging like a sack of potatoes.

The man with the horribly disfigured face ruined by disease or radiation burns laughs and says, "A good day's work. Kali will be well pleased."

Kali! Now you remember. Kali, the ancient Hindu goddess—and her cult of death and destruction.

Kali lives! But you and the shuttle crew will not.

The End

The first night on the plains is a harsh one. Not only are you cold and hungry, but you can't sleep. Big cats—much like lions—are nearby. You can hear them roaring on both sides of the tent. You lie in your sleeping bag, hour after hour, tense and fearful, clutching your spear, never knowing when one of the animals will leap on you.

You're weary but grateful when the sky turns dull red and the huge, dim sun begins to rise over the plain. Today maybe you'll spear a dohkoe.

Turn to page 41.

Bob Walker, the helmsman, and Nan Pacella elect to go with the captain. As the three of them are herded toward the shuttle, Barnes slaps a hand on your shoulder. "Will you be staying with us, matey, or do you want to *die* out in space with Captain Tyler? Decide, now!"

You glance at the captain. His stern eyes meet yours.

"If you stay, you'll hang with the rest of them!" the captain says.

"Well?" Barnes jabs a finger into your stomach. "Will you go or stay?"

If you decide to go with Captain Tyler in the shuttle craft, turn to page 8.

If you stay on the Baruna *with the mutineers, turn to page 2.*

The next crew member you meet is the navigator, Nan Pacella. She's a slender woman with dark hair and intelligent eyes. Nan shows you around the ship and introduces you to Jack Barnes, the first mate. Barnes is tall and lean. His handsome face is marked by a scar that runs the length of his right jaw.

He looks you over, up and down, and grips your hand so hard it hurts. "Welcome aboard, matey," he bellows in a hearty voice. He smiles broadly at you, but for some reason his grin seems more menacing than friendly.

"Watch out for him," Nan says when Barnes is out of earshot. "Don't let his smile fool you. He's left deeper marks than that scar on his face on those who've crossed him."

Turn to page 100.

A second later the captain joins you. Inside, Nan and Walker greet you warmly, glad you're alive.

But what do we do now? you wonder. The captain, echoing your thought, asks the same question out loud. "We're still too low on fuel and food to get to a habitable planet," he adds.

The young man you saved smiles at each of you. "Do you have enough fuel and food for a two-day journey?" he asks.

"Yes," you say cautiously.

"Then we have no problem," he says. "I can guide you away from Kali—to Dompuss, and safety."

The captain looks at you as if asking for your help.

Dompuss? Why not? you think. It can't be any worse than Kali.

"What are we waiting for," you say. "Let's set course for Dompuss!"

The End

ABOUT THE AUTHORS

EDWARD PACKARD is a graduate of Princeton University and Columbia Law School. He developed the unique storytelling approach used in the Choose Your Own Adventure series while thinking up stories for his children, Caroline, Andrea, and Wells.

R.A. MONTGOMERY is a graduate of Williams College and also studied in graduate programs at Yale University and New York University. After serving in a variety of administrative capacities at Williston Academy and Columbia University, he co-founded Waitsfield Summer School in 1965. Following that, Montgomery helped found a research and development firm specializing in the development of educational programs. He worked for several years as a consultant to the Peace Corps in Washington, D.C., and West Africa.

ABOUT THE ILLUSTRATOR

HOWARD BENDER is the creator and illustrator of the *MR. FIXITT* series (Apple Comics) and has illustrated *THE HONEYMOONERS: AN ILLUSTRATED TRIVIA BOOK,* the *TELL ME WHY* series, and a number of comic books and coloring books. He lives in Toms River, New Jersey, with his wife and two children, Justin and Nicholas.

CHOOSE YOUR OWN ADVENTURE

Special Offer
Buy a Bantam Book
for only 50¢.

Now you can order the exciting books you've been wanting to read straight from Bantam's latest catalog of hundreds of titles. *And* this special offer gives you the opportunity to purchase a Bantam book for only 50¢. Here's how:

By ordering any five books at the regular price per order, you can also choose any other single book listed (up to a $5.95 value) for only 50¢. Some restrictions do apply, so for further details send for Bantam's catalog of titles today.

Just send us your name and address and we'll send you Bantam Book's SHOP AT HOME CATALOG!